PINGU

Annual 1995

This book belongs to

_____

Contents

Written by Brenda Apsley
Illustrated by Jo Davies and Jane Swift
Designed by Andrew Maddock

Published in Great Britain by World International, an imprint of Egmont Publishing Ltd., Egmont House, PO Box 111, Great Ducie Street, Manchester M60 3BL.
Printed in Great Britain. ISBN 0 7498 2020 9

All about Pingu

This is Pingu.
He is a penguin who lives in a cold land where everything is covered in ice and snow.
It is called the South Pole.

Pingu lives in an igloo, a house made of blocks of snow. He lives with his family. Mama looks after his baby sister, Pinga. Papa delivers letters on his post sledge. Sometimes Pingu helps him. Pingu's grandpa lives in his own igloo a little way away. He is teaching Pingu how to play the accordion.

Pingu goes to school. So do his friends Ping, Pingo and Pingi. Pingi always wants to sit next to Pingu. She likes him very much.

Living at the South Pole is lots of fun. Pingu catches fish with his friend Robby the seal. He rides down icy hills on his ice scooter and his sledge. He can skate, too.

Greedy Pingu

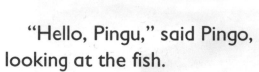

Pingu had had a very busy morning. He had
gone out very early to the ice hole with his
fishing pole and a big red bucket of seaweed
for bait. He had caught lots and lots of fish
and was taking them home in the bucket
when he met his friends Pingo and Pingi.

"Hello, Pingu," said Pingo,
looking at the fish.
"Did you catch all those?"
Pingu yawned. He was tired.
"Yes, every one," he said.
"They're all mine."
Pingi looked at the fish, too. "You are clever,
Pingu," she said. "They look really tasty."
Pingu took a fish from the bucket and ate it in
three big beakfuls. "Yes, they are tasty," he said.
"Very." He ate another one just as fast.

Pingi couldn't take his eyes off the fish. It was a
few hours since he had eaten his breakfast and he
was hungry. He hoped Pingu would give him a fish,
but Pingu didn't. Instead, he ate a third fish.
"Could I have one?" asked Pingo.
"Me too?" said Pingi. "Just a little one?"
Pingu shook his head. "No!" he said. "No, I'm
going to eat them all myself." Pingo and Pingi
watched as he ate fish number four in two bites.

"Oh, please, Pingu," said Pingo. "Just one each. You'll still have lots of fish left."

"No!" said Pingu. "They're mine, all mine." He ate fish number six, fish number seven, and fish number eight.

Pingi watched. She was feeling very hungry now. "Could Pingo and I share a fish, Pingu?" she asked. "Please."

Pingu took a fish from the bucket and held it by its tail. He put it near Pingi's beak, but just as she was about to bite it he pulled it away and ate it himself. That was nine fish he had eaten.

"What a mean thing to do!" said Pingi.

"Don't care!" said Pingu. "I caught them all and I'm going to eat them all, so there!" and he ate fish number ten.

"Come on, Pingi," said Pingo. "Let him eat them all. We'll go and catch our own."

Pingu walked off towards home. On the way he ate five more fish. His bucket was nearly empty now.

When Pingu got home he wasn't feeling very well. His tummy was very full and starting to hurt. "I feel sick," he told Mama.

"What have you been eating?" she asked.

"Fish," said Pingu. He was starting to turn a very funny green colour. "Fifteen of them."

"FIFTEEN?" said Mama. "Oh, you silly, greedy penguin, Pingu."

But Pingu didn't hear her. He rushed into the bathroom holding his wing over his mouth. He was very sick.

Mama put Pingu to bed for the rest of the day. He felt very miserable and his tummy still hurt.

When Papa came home he was surprised to see Pingu in bed. "Pingu hasn't been feeling very well," Mama explained.

"I'm sorry to hear that," said Papa. He took a big box out of his bag. "Would a big piece of my ice-cream cake cheer you up?" he asked. He took the lid off the box and held the cake under Pingu's nose.

Pingu closed his eyes. He turned that funny green colour again. He shook his head and pulled the covers over his head with a groan.

Later on Pingu was feeling a little bit better. Papa sat beside his bed and Pingu told him all about the fish he had caught and eaten.

He told him about not sharing the fish with Pingo and Pingi, too.

"Oh," said Papa. "That wasn't the right thing to do, was it?"

"No," said Pingu. He had had a lot of time to think about it. Two big tears rolled down his beak. "It was mean. If I had shared the fish I wouldn't have eaten so many myself. And I wouldn't have had a sore tummy and been sick." More tears rolled down his beak. "And Pingi and Pingo would still be friends with me."

Papa had an idea. He dried Pingu's tears and whispered to him. Pingu nodded his head. It was a good idea.

The next morning Pingu was feeling much better.

At school he went over to Pingo and Pingi. Even Pingi didn't look very pleased to see him.

"Well?" said Pingo. "What do you want?" He was angry with Pingu.

"I want to say I'm sorry," said Pingu. "I should have shared my fish with you. It was mean not to."

Pingu looked so sad that Pingo and Pingi couldn't stay cross with him. "Shall we be friends again?" asked Pingi.

Pingu nodded. "Please," he said. He took two paper parcels out of his school bag. "It's Papa's ice-cream cake. A big slice for each of you."

"Thank you, Pingu," said Pingo. Papa's cake was famous.

"But where's your piece?" asked Pingi.

Pingu had forgotten to cut a piece for himself. "Oh, I forgot," he said.

"It doesn't matter," said Pingi. "You can share ours!"

Papa's post sledge

Pingu likes to help Papa load letters
and parcels on his post sledge.

Look at the pictures carefully.
Five things have disappeared in the bottom picture.
Can you say what they are?

The answers are on page 61.

Where are they?

Professor Threehorn is very absent-minded. He puts things away, then forgets where he has put them. He has lost five of his books.

"Can you help me find them, Pingu?"

Look carefully – Professor Threehorn has put his books in some VERY odd places!

The answers are on page 61.

Make a Pingu jigsaw

Do you like doing jigsaws?
Pingu does.
One day Mama showed him
how to make his own jigsaw.
Why don't you
make one too?

Draw and colour
a picture of Pingu.
Copy the one on
this page, or make
up your own.

Ask a grown-up to cut a piece of
card for you. It should be the same
size and shape as your picture. Mama
cut up Pingu's empty cereal packet.

Spread glue on one side of the card.
Press your picture on top.
Wait until the glue is dry.

On the back of the card, draw lines to make triangles, rectangles and squares. Pingu used a ruler and pencil so his lines were straight.

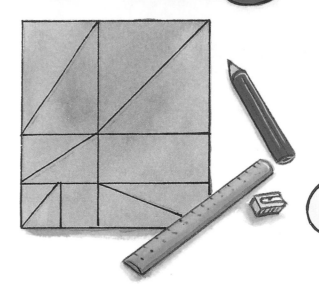

Ask a grown-up to help you cut along the lines. When you have finished you will have lots of little jigsaw pieces.

Can you fit the jigsaw pieces together to make the picture again?

The ski track

Pingu and Pingo like skiing. They are going to have a race to see who will be first to the end of the ski track.

You and a friend can race with them. You can be Pingu and your friend can be Pingo. You need a counter each and a die.

Start at the red flag. Take turns to throw the die. Move your counter from flag to flag. If you shake two, move two flags, and so on until one of you crosses the finishing line.

If you land on a **BLACK** flag you must miss a turn.

If you land on a **GREEN** flag you have an extra throw.

Ice games

1. It was a special day at school. The children were going to play ice games and sports, and take part in races. Their parents had come to watch.

2. Pingu couldn't wait for things to start. He was good at ice games. "I'm going to win everything," he said. "Just watch me!"

3. In the skating race Pingu started the last lap in the lead. "Catch me if you can!" he said to Ping as they went around the last corner.

4. Oh, no! Pingu didn't see the stone on the ice. He skidded and crossed the finishing line on his bottom! "Pingu is disqualified!" said the teacher.

5. The skiing race was next. Pingu had waxed his skis and was sure he would win. He set off as soon as the teacher said, "Ready, set, go!"

6. Pingu flew down the hill. He swished this way and that, zigzagging around the flags. He was going much faster than the other racers.

7. Near the finishing line Pingu looked at his parents to make sure they were watching him. He didn't look where he was going and...

8. Pingu missed the last flag and skied right off the track. The tip of his ski got caught in a net and Pingu flew into the air.

9. Over and over he turned, then *plop*! *thud*! he landed head first in a big pile of snow. Pingu's feet and skis were all that could be seen.

10. The teacher and Papa had to dig Pingu out of the snow. "Are you ready for the ice hockey game?" asked the teacher. Pingu nodded. "Yes."

11. The score was one goal each in the ice hockey game when Pingu got the puck. He went for a big hit with his stick, but missed the puck.

12. Pingu went into a tight spin. Faster and faster he went, round and round. When he stopped he was very dizzy. The teacher helped him off the pitch.

13. Pingu soon felt better and got ready for the ice skating contest. Things had not gone well at all but he was determined to win something.

14. Pingu skated very well. He did jumps and spins, leaps and turns. But in his last spin his skates touched and he flew into the air.

15. Pingu had been going so fast that he soared up and flew over the heads of the spectators and right out of the skating rink.

16. This time Pingu didn't land in a pile of soft snow. No, this time Pingu landed with a huge splash in a fishing hole cut in the ice.

17. Pingu was cold and wet when Papa helped him out of the water. The teacher gave him some hot tea and wrapped him in a warm blanket.

18. When the prizes were being given out Pingu stood with Mama and Papa. He was very disappointed. "Everyone won something except me," he said.

19. "Never mind," said Mama. "You tried hard." Just then Pingi came over to where they were standing. "I made this for you, Pingu," she said.

20. It was a medal made of silver foil. "You didn't win anything, but I still think you're the best," Pingi said. Pingu blushed bright red!

Papa's workshed

Papa has set a puzzle for Pingu and Ping to try. "Can you find ten things in my workshed that begin with the letter sound s?" Papa asks.

Can you help Pingu and Ping find them all?

The answers are on page 61.

Snowflakes

Pingu and Pinga were looking at snowflakes with Grandpa. When they looked through his big magnifying glass the snowflakes looked as big as saucers.
"No two snowflakes are exactly the same," said Grandpa.
"But they all have six points."

Pingu counted them.
"One, two, three, four, five, six," he said.
"You're right, Grandpa."
Grandpa showed Pingu and Pinga how to make paper snowflakes.
Why don't you try making some too?

You need some white paper. Get some help to draw a circle on the paper. You could draw round a saucer or small plate. Cut out the circle. "Always use safety scissors with round ends," says Pingu.

Fold the paper circle in half. Now make a fold on each side. Now you have a cone shape. The pictures will help you.

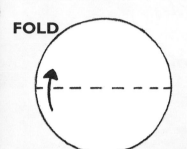
FOLD

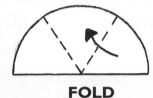
FOLD

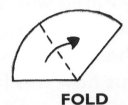
FOLD

Cut the pointed top off the cone. Cut small triangles of paper from the sides and base of the cone. Don't cut right across from one side to the other.

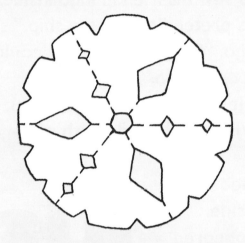

Open out the paper carefully to see your snowflake. You can stick it on to darker paper to show the pattern.

Pinga collected all the paper scraps and threw them into the air. "It's snowing!" said Pinga.

Let's pretend

One day Pingu was outside the igloo when he saw something moving towards him across the ice. It was a big chest made of wood. But how was it moving, thought Pingu: "Chests don't have legs."

The chest stopped near Papa's workshed. Pingu walked all around it. Then he heard a voice from inside the chest saying something like, 'Met me mout'. But how could it speak, thought Pingu: "Chests can't speak."

Pingu lifted one side of the chest and saw his friend Pingo inside. "I was pretending to be a ship," said Pingo. "But once I got in I couldn't get out again."

"It's a big chest," said Pingu. "What shall we do with it?"

"Let's pretend it's a submarine," said Pingo. They turned the chest over and climbed inside. "Up periscope," said Pingo. Pingu's head appeared over the edge of the chest. "Up penguinscope, you mean!" said Pingu. "Dive! Dive!"

Along came Pinga. "Can I play?" she asked.

"No, go away," said Pingu. "This is a game for brave sailors, not babies."

"Let's pretend it's a plane now," said Pingo, who was full of ideas.

"Yes," said Pingu, who had some ideas of his own. "Wait here." He came back with two of his red woolly hats and some snow goggles. "Put them on, Pingo. Now we look like real pilots."

Pingu and Pingo held their wings out and pretended to fly the plane. "Voom! Voom!" said Pingu. "Ready for take-off!"

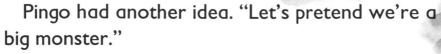

Their game was interrupted by Pinga again. "I want to play," she said. "It's not fair. Let me."

"GO AWAY," said Pingu. "NOW. This is a game for brave pilots, not babies."

Pingo had another idea. "Let's pretend we're a big monster."

They turned the chest over and held it above their heads. They walked around the shed to where Pinga was playing with her bricks.

"Grrrrrr!" growled the monster. "Grrroan!"

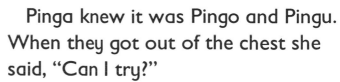

Pinga knew it was Pingo and Pingu. When they got out of the chest she said, "Can I try?"

"All right," said Pingu. "But I told you, this is not a game for babies."

Pinga got inside the chest and tried to make some monster noises of her own.

Pingu and Pingo looked at each other. They both had the same idea. "Shall we?" said Pingo.

"Yes!" said Pingu.

They banged on the sides of the chest and shouted and yelled. It was very dark inside the chest and Pinga was frightened. "Let me out," she said in a small voice. "Please, Pingu."

But Pingu and Pingo kept on banging and shouting.

"Please let me out," said Pinga. This time she sounded as if she might start to cry soon.

Pingo and Pingu lifted the side of the chest and Pinga crawled out. She ran off towards the igloo.

"Let's pretend to be something else," said Pingu. "Pinga might tell Mama about the monster, and then we'll be in trouble."

"Let's pretend the chest is a train," said Pingo.

"Yes," said Pingu. "There's one of Papa's old caps in the workshed. It will make a good train driver's cap. Let's go and find it."

When they came out of the workshed a few minutes later Pingu and Pingo heard a voice. "Ahoy there!" it said.

They looked around. The chest had gone!

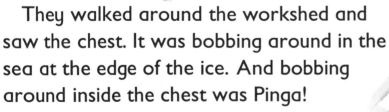

They walked around the workshed and saw the chest. It was bobbing around in the sea at the edge of the ice. And bobbing around inside the chest was Pinga!

"Do you like my boat?" cried Pinga.

"Oh, no," said Pingu. "How will we get her back? And what will Mama say?"

The chest was starting to float away from the ice edge. "Help!" shouted Pingu. "Help, someone!"

A sleek grey head popped up in the water. It was Pingu's seal friend, Robby. "What's wrong?" he asked.

Pingu pointed to the chest. "Over there. The chest is floating away, and Pinga is inside it."

"No problem," said Robby. He dived under the water and came up again behind the chest. He swam to the shore, pushing the chest in front of him with his nose.

When the chest was up against the edge of the ice they pulled Pinga to safety. She didn't realize she had been in danger. "That was a good game!" she said.

"Thank you, Robby," said Pingu. "I think I'll take Pinga home now." Pingu was so glad that his sister was safe and he felt guilty for not looking after her properly.

When they got home Mama asked what they had been doing all afternoon.

Pingu looked worried. "Erm, nothing much," he said. "We were just playing pretend, erm..."

"Well you can tell me all about it over tea," said Mama.

Imagine

Do you play pretend games like Pingu and his friends?
Do you imagine things?

Sometimes the things we imagine are exciting. How do you feel when you go to bed on Christmas Eve and think about the gifts Santa Claus will bring?

Sometimes the things we imagine are scary. How do you think Pinga felt inside the dark chest when Pingu and Pingo were shouting and banging on the sides?

Look at these pictures.
They show something Pingu imagined.
How do you think he felt in each picture?

Pingu's word square

"Can you find these ten words in my word square?
I have written them up and down and from side to side.
Draw a line around each word when you find it and
tick the box below."

A	B	M	S	K	I	K	L
G	R	A	N	D	P	A	X
Y	O	P	O	P	I	N	G
I	B	Q	W	O	N	N	I
C	B	B	M	N	G	U	G
E	Y	H	A	E	A	P	L
J	I	C	M	U	F	S	O
P	A	P	A	G	R	T	O

☐ GRANDPA   ☐ PAPA   ☐ SKI

☐ ICE   ☐ PING   ☐ SNOW

☐ IGLOO   ☐ PINGA

☐ MAMA   ☐ ROBBY

The answers are on page 61.

Heave!

Tug of war

Play this tug of war game with a friend.
You need a counter each, and a die.

Put your counters on the yellow **START** knot
in the middle of the rope.

Take turns to throw the die.

If you throw a 1, a 2 or a 3,
move your counter one knot to the **LEFT**.

If you throw a 4, a 5 or a 6,
move your counter one knot to the **RIGHT**.

The first one to reach the **WIN** end
at the right of the rope is the winner.

Start here!

LEFT

START

Old King Cold

Pingu is having fun making up new words for favourite nursery rhymes.

He sings the first one to the tune of **Old King Cole**. Why don't you sing it with him?

Old King Cold was a snowy old seal
And a snowy old seal was he.
He called for his fish
And he called for his skis
And he called for his skaters three.

Sing the next rhyme to the tune of Baa, baa black sheep.

"Waark, waark, Robby,
Have you any fish?"

"Honk! Yes, Pingu,
In my little dish."

Pingu's igloo

Pingu has been busy. He has cut lots of blocks of ice and used them to build an igloo.

He has one more piece to choose to finish the igloo. Only one will fit. Can you help him find it?

A

B

C

D

E

F

The answers are on page 61.

Pingu pretends

"Wake up, sleepyhead," Mama said to Pingu one morning. "It's time to get ready for school."

But Pingu was in a bad mood. He didn't want to get up and he didn't want to go to school. He pulled the blankets over his head.

Mama pulled them off again. "Come on, Pingu," she said. "Hurry."

But Pingu really didn't want to get up and go to school. He had an idea. "I've got tummy ache," he said in a quiet little voice. "It hurts." It didn't really – Pingu was pretending.

"Poor Pingu," said Mama, stroking his head. "No school for you today, then. Stay in bed and rest and when I've given Pinga her breakfast I'll come and see how you are."

While Mama sat at the table with her back to Pingu he crept to the kitchen cupboard and took out a squeezy bottle of tomato ketchup. He squirted little spots of ketchup all over his face and jumped back into bed.

When Mama saw the spots she was worried. "Lie quietly, Pingu," she said, kissing the top of his head. "I'm going to the doctor's surgery. I'll be back soon."

When Mama came back Pingu was reading a comic. Mama took it away. "No reading for you," she said. "You'll tire yourself."

Mama put a big bottle of green medicine beside the bed. She poured some into a big spoon. "Open wide, Pingu," she said.

The medicine smelled awful and tasted even worse.

"It will do you good," said Mama. "You have to take one more spoonful now, and another in an hour's time. Open wide again."

"I don't like it!" said Pingu, but as he opened his beak Mama poured the medicine in quickly. The second spoonful tasted worse than the first. Pingu pulled a face.

"It will do you good," Mama said again.

Pingu wasn't so sure. "Can I play with some toys?" Pingu asked.

"No," said Mama. "Just lie quietly and rest."

Pingu's plan was not working out. He couldn't play. He couldn't read. He was stuck in bed with nothing to do. And he could still taste that awful green medicine.

Next time Mama came with the medicine Pingu was ready. He let her put it into his mouth but as she turned her back he reached under the bed and brought out Pinga's potty. He spat the medicine into the potty. "Yuk!" he said. "Horrible stuff!"

Pingu had a miserable morning. He tossed and turned. He tried to sleep, but he wasn't tired. He stared at the ceiling. He stared at the walls. He counted all the cracks he could see, but got bored when he got to thirty.

He watched Pinga as she played and wished he could play, too. He even wished he was at school.

Pingu watched hungrily when Mama and a neighbour sat down to eat their lunch.

The fish smelled delicious. "Mama, I'm hungry," said Pingu. His tummy felt empty.

"Sorry, Pingu," said Mama. "The doctor said you shouldn't have any food today."

"What, nothing at all?" said Pingu. "All day? But I didn't even have any breakfast."

"I know," said Mama. "The doctor said you can start eating tomorrow. But only if those spots have gone and you feel better."

Pingu put his head under the blanket. He wiped off the tomato ketchup with his wing and licked it. He put his head out again. "Look, Mama, my spots have gone," he said. "And I feel much better. Can I have some lunch?"

Mama shook her head. "No, Pingu," she said. "But it's time for more medicine. Open wide."

Pingu groaned. What a day!

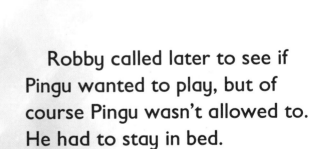

Robby called later to see if Pingu wanted to play, but of course Pingu wasn't allowed to. He had to stay in bed.

When Papa came in that night he was surprised to see Pingu in bed. "Haven't you been to school today?" he asked.

Pingu shook his head. "No, I didn't feel very well. But I'm better now."

"So you missed the visit to the ice caves," said Papa. "What a shame."

Pingu groaned. "Oh, no!" he said. He had been looking forward to the school trip for ages. He had forgotten it was today. While he had been lying in bed, bored, fed up and having only horrible green medicine to drink, his friends had been having fun at the ice caves. Pingu looked very sad. "It's not fair," he said.

Mama tucked him in. "I think you're much better now," she said. "Do you think you'll be well enough to go to school tomorrow?"

Pingu thought of the miserable day he had had.

"Oh, yes, Mama," he said. "Oh, yes! And I'm never going to be ill again, I promise!"

Guess who-Pingu!

Who do you think Pingu is pretending to be in the pictures below?

1

2

3

4

5

The answers are on page 61.

Make a Pingu bookmark

This Pingu bookmark really talks! Here's how to make it.

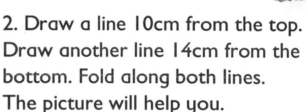

1. Ask a grown-up to help you cut out a strip of white paper about 27cm long and 6cm wide.

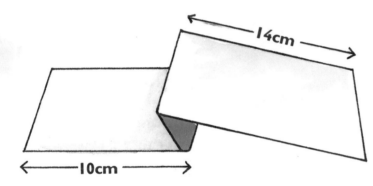

2. Draw a line 10cm from the top. Draw another line 14cm from the bottom. Fold along both lines. The picture will help you.

3. Now you have a folded paper strip 21cm long. Draw Pingu's head and the top half of his beak on the top part. Draw the rest of him on the bottom part. The fold should be where his mouth is, like this:

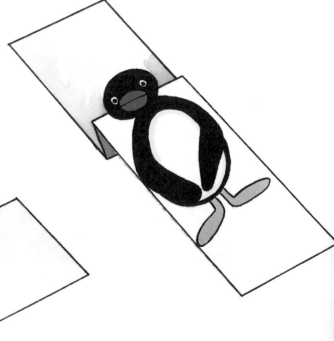

4. Open up the folds and finish drawing Pingu, his mouth wide open. Colour your picture.

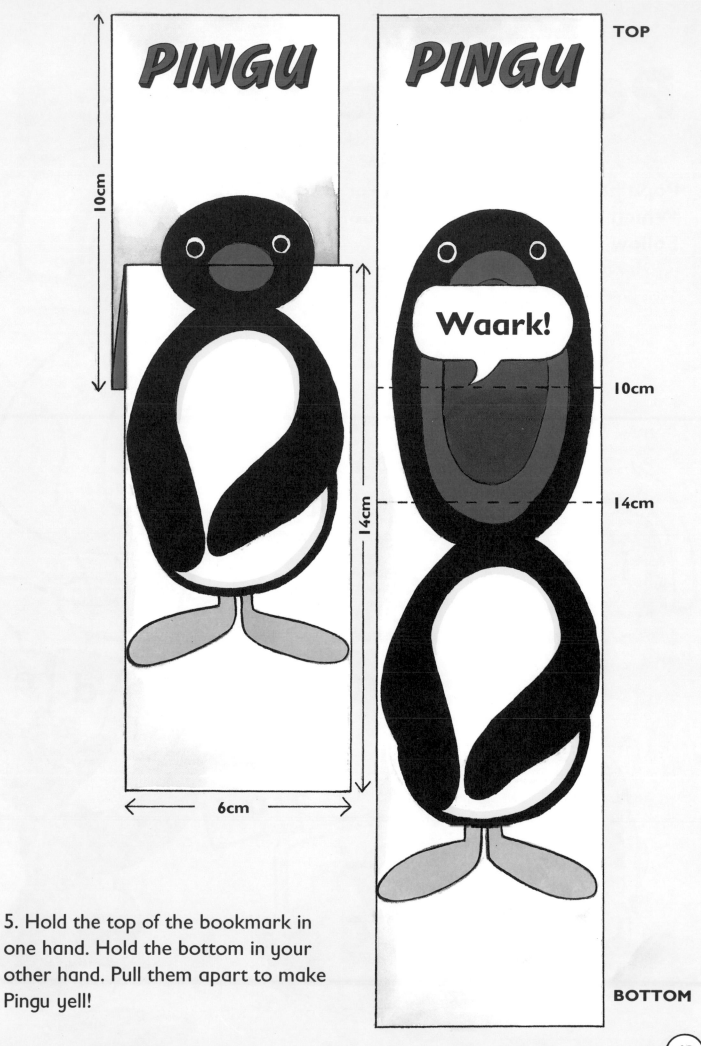

5. Hold the top of the bookmark in one hand. Hold the bottom in your other hand. Pull them apart to make Pingu yell!

Papa's letters

Papa has lots of letters to deliver.
Which letter goes to which igloo?
Follow the lines to find out.

The answers are on page 61.

Pingu paints a picture

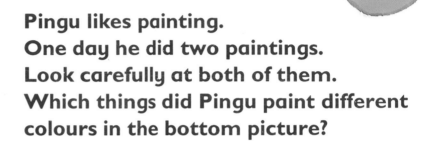

Pingu likes painting.
One day he did two paintings.
Look carefully at both of them.
Which things did Pingu paint different colours in the bottom picture?

The answers are on page 61.

45

Pingu in the kitchen

1. Mama was busy in the kitchen one day. She was making Pingu and Pinga's favourite food – pancakes. "Can I help, Mama?" asked Pingu.

2. Mama gave Pingu a big mixing bowl. He put some flour into the bowl then looked into the flour bag to see if there was any left inside.

3. When Pingu pulled his head out of the bag it was covered with flour. He was all white. He did look funny! Pinga giggled.

4. Pingu broke an egg into the flour and mixed in some milk. He stirred the batter with a big wooden spoon, faster and faster, faster and faster.

5. Bits of batter started to fly out of the mixing bowl. Soon Pingu and Pinga were covered in yellow spots. "Look at you!" Pingu said to Pinga.

6. "And look at you!" Mama said to Pingu. "What a mess!" She wiped the batter off Pingu and Pinga with a wet cloth. Pingu didn't like having his face wiped.

7. Mama gave Pingu an apron to wear. He started mixing again. "I want to help! I want to help! Let me!" said Pinga, pulling at the apron.

8. Pingu had an idea. A naughty idea. "You can help by holding these eggs for me," he said. Pinga held the eggs one in each wing.

47

9. Pingu waited a while then said, "Clap wings, Pinga!" Pinga did just that. Clap! Crack! Splat! Pinga's wings were covered in runny egg.

10. Mama wasn't very pleased. "Either help properly or go away," she said. "Take the frying pan. You start the pancakes while I clean Pinga up."

11. Pingu poured some batter into the frying pan. When it was cooked he flipped the pancake up into the air. Up and up went the pancake...

12. ...but it didn't come down again. Pingu looked at the empty frying pan. Where could it be? He looked under the table and in the mixing bowl.

13. Pingu looked on the book shelf and behind the cushions on the sofa. He couldn't find the pancake anywhere. Pinga looked in her potty.

14. Pingu gave up and cooked another pancake. He flipped it into the air. Up and up it went...but this one didn't come down, either!

15. Pingu searched for the pancake. Do you know where he found it? On top of Papa's head! Papa was fast alseep in his chair and didn't notice!

16. Pingu peeled the pancake off Papa's head without waking him. "Don't tell him, Mama," said Pingu. Mama agreed; it was an accident, after all.

17. Mama helped Pingu and Pinga make the rest of the pancakes. Soon there was a tall pile of pancakes. Pingu carried them to the table.

18. "Mmmm, these are good pancakes," said Papa. "You know, I had a very strange dream earlier. Can you guess what it was about?"

19. Mama and Pingu looked at each other in alarm. They shook their heads. No, they couldn't guess. "It was about a pancake!" said Papa.

20. Just then the lost pancake landed with a *plop*! on Pingu's head! It had stuck on the ceiling. "The one place I didn't look!" said Pingu.

A meal for Mama

**Pingu is helping Papa cook the evening meal for Mama.
Can you guess what they are having to eat?**

Look at the picture carefully.

The answers are on page 61.

Snowballs

Pingu and his friends love making snowballs and throwing them at each other.
Pingu knows how to make snowballs you can eat, too. Why don't you try making some?

You need a block of white marzipan and some desiccated coconut.

You need clean hands, too.

Ask a grown-up to help you cut the marzipan into about 20 small pieces.

Roll each piece into a ball shape between your hands.

Put some water on a plate or saucer.

Put the desiccated coconut on another plate or saucer.

Dip the marzipan balls into the water, then roll them in the coconut. Roll them until the marzipan is covered in coconut.

Eat your snowballs!

Yummy!

Scrummy!

53

Ski track maze

Pingu is at the top of the hill.
He wants to ski down to the cabin,
but he isn't sure which ski track will take him there.
Can you help him choose the right one?

a
b
c
d
e

The answers are on page 61.

Pingu's jokes page

What is a mermaid, Pingu?

A deep she fish?

What happened when the penguin sat on a pin?
Nothing – it was a safety pin!

What animal with two humps would you find at the South Pole?
A lost camel?

What do you call a penguin with a seagull on his head?
Cliff!

What do you call a clever penguin?
Birdbrain!

What is white and travels upwards?
A silly snowflake.

What do you call a penguin wearing ear muffs?
Anything you like – he won't be able to hear you!

Knock, knock.
Who's there?
Snow.
Snow who?
Snow use, I've forgotten his name.

The babysitter

One evening Mama and Papa were going out to a concert. Grandpa had come to babysit.
Just before they left, Mama spoke to Grandpa. "I'm sure Pingu and Pinga won't be any trouble. They are both tired. I think they'll be ready for bed soon."

But Pingu and Pinga had other ideas. They loved Grandpa because he was always ready to play with them. He was great fun.
"Would you like to play a game before bedtime?" asked Grandpa.
"Yes! Yes!" said Pingu. "You be a horse, Grandpa, and we'll be rodeo riders."
Grandpa got down on the floor and Pingu and Pinga jumped up on to his back. He bucked and reared up just like a real wild west horse and Pingu and Pinga had to hold on tight.

Pinga and Pingu laughed so much. They weren't tired at all, and went off to look for ideas for other games. Grandpa had a rest while they were gone.

In the bathroom Pinga found Mama's talcum powder. She dipped the big fluffy puff into the tub and soon she was covered in white powder. "You look like a snow monster!" said Pingu, and soon he was white, too.

"Roarrrr!" said Pingu, waving his wings about.

"Roarrrr!" said Pinga, copying him.

"Arrrrgh!" said Grandpa. "Monsters!" And he rushed off to hide behind Papa's chair.

"Are you two ready for bed yet?" asked Grandpa as he dusted off the talcum powder. He yawned.

"No, not yet. Another game, Grandpa!" said Pingu. He went into the kitchen and came back with two big pans and some wooden spoons.

Pingu put one pan on his head and the other on Grandpa's. "Viking helmets," Pingu explained, and handed Grandpa a lid. "And shields." He gave Grandpa a wooden spoon, too. "That's your Viking sword," he explained.

"I want a helmet! I want a sword!" said Pinga.

Pingu looked around. He found Pinga's potty, put it on her head and gave her a little spoon. "There you are," he said.

Pingu and Pinga fought Grandpa. "Take that!" said Pingu, pushing the wooden spoon into Grandpa's tummy.

"And that!" said Pinga, using her spoon.

Grandpa dropped his shield and sword and clutched his tummy. "You win, you nasty Vikings," he groaned, and fell to the floor.

He didn't move, even when Pinga shook him. "Grandpa," she said. "Grandpa, it was only pretend fighting."

Still Grandpa didn't move.

He was a good actor.

Pinga looked as if she was about to cry when he suddenly leapt up and roared a loud Viking roar. He grabbed his wooden spoon, and chased her around the room until he had to stop to get his breath back.

Pinga was frightened and excited at the same time. "More! More!" she said.

Grandpa yawned a big yawn. He was tired, but Pingu and Pinga weren't. Pingu had already thought of another game.

Pingu used string to tie a cushion to his tummy. He did the same for Grandpa and Pingu.

"What are we going to play now?" asked Grandpa.

Pingu rushed at Grandpa, fat tummy to fat tummy. They bounced apart and Pingu fell on to his back like an upturned turtle. "Sumo wrestling!" said Pingu.

Grandpa, Pingu and Pinga bounced and bumped around the room until Grandpa flopped down into Papa's chair. "I'm getting too old for this," he said. "Time for bed."

"Oh, no!" said Pinga, jumping up on his knee. "Just one more game, PLEASE, Grandpa."

"All right, one more game," said Grandpa. He rubbed his eyes. "What is it this time?"

Pinga ran to the toy box. She came back with curly orange wigs and a big red nose. "They're what circus clowns wear," she said. "We got them for Christmas."

Pingu pretended he was the ring master. "The Pingu Circus proudly presents the famous juggler," he said, "The Great Grandpapee!"

Pingu and Pinga clapped and cheered. Grandpa tried to juggle with three balls but he wasn't very good and kept on dropping the balls.

Grandpa went off for a rest while Pingu and Pinga pretended to throw buckets of water over each other.

When Mama and Papa came home from the concert Pingu and Pinga were sitting on the floor playing Snap.

"I thought you two would be in bed by now," said Papa. "It's late."

Mama looked around. "And where is Grandpa?"

Pingu pointed. Grandpa was lying, fast asleep on Pingu's bed.

He was still wearing the curly orange wig and the big red nose on the end of his beak. Pinga's teddy bear was in his arms.

"Next time we'll let you two babysit Grandpa!" said Papa. "Come on, time for bed!"

Answers to puzzles

Page 10 Papa's post sledge

A parcel, Papa's cap, the Post Office manager's glasses, the door knob and the headlamp from the front of the post sledge have all disappeared.

Page 11 Where are they?

Page 21 Papa's workshed

String, shoe, skis, screwdriver, seashell, saw, scissors, shelf and spade all begin with **s**. Sack does, too.

Page 29 Pingu's word square

Page 35 Pingu's igloo

Piece **c** will fit.

Page 41 Guess who - Pingu!

Pingu is dressed as: **1.** a snowman, **2.** Papa, **3.** a sailor, **4.** Pingu's teacher, **5.** a snowball.

Page 44 Papa's letters

a3, b5, c1, d2, e4

Page 45 Pingu paints a picture

The books, shelf, radio, picture frame, table, sun in the picture, Pinga's feet and her beak are different colours.

Page 51 A meal for Mama

For the evening meal they will have: potatoes, peas, fish, tomatoes, lettuce, bread and butter, cakes, and orange juice.

Page 54 Ski track maze

Track **d** leads to the cabin.

61